My mother, Barbara, always read stories to me when I was little. At bedtime we'd travel to all the secret places in the world, through books.

We both make up our own stories now, and Barbara says she gets her best ideas in the bath. Tashi began in the bath, and we talked him into life—and into this book—together. Anna Fienberg

Anna Fienberg is well known for her imaginative children's books, including *The Magnificent Nose and Other Marvels* and *The Hottest Boy Who Ever Lived*, both of which are illustrated by Kim Gamble.

Kim is one of Australia's leading illustrators for children. His other books include *Come the Terrible Tiger* and *Dear Fred*.

Anna Fienberg would like to thank the Literature
Board of the Australia Council for their assistance.

First published in 1995

Allen & Unwin
83 Alexander Street,
Crows Nest NSW 2065 Australia
Phone: (61 2) 8425 0100
Fax: (61 2) 9906 2218
E-mail: info@allenandunwin.com
Web: www.allenandunwin.com

National Library of Australia
Cataloguing-in-Publication entry:

Fienberg, Anna.
Tashi.

ISBN 1 86373 806 1.

I. Fienberg, Barbara. II. Gamble, Kim.
III. Title.

A823.3

Typeset in Sabon by P.I.X.E.L. Pty Ltd, Melbourne
Printed in Australia by McPherson's Printing Group

15 14 13 12 11 10

Tashi

written by
**Anna
Fienberg**

and

**Barbara
Fienberg**

illustrated by
Kim Gamble

ALLEN & UNWIN

'I have a new friend,' said Jack one night
at dinner.
'Oh, good,' said Mum. 'What's his name?'
'Tashi, and he comes from a place very far
away.'

'That's interesting,' said Dad.

'Yes,' said Jack. 'He came here on a swan.'

'A black or white swan?' asked Dad.

'It doesn't *matter,*' said Jack. 'You always ask the wrong questions!'

'How did Tashi get here on a swan then?' asked Mum.

'Well,' said Jack, 'it was like this. Tashi's parents were very poor. They wanted to come to this country, but they didn't have enough money for the air fare. So they had to sell Tashi to a war lord to buy the tickets.'

'How much did the tickets cost?' asked Dad.

'It doesn't *matter*,' said Jack. 'You always ask the wrong questions!'

'So why is Tashi here, and not with the war lord?' asked Mum.

'Well,' said Jack, 'it was like this. Soon after Tashi's mother and father left, he was crying for them down by a lake. A swan heard his cries and told him to jump on his back. The swan flew many days and nights until he arrived here, right at the front door of Tashi's parents' new house.'

'Did he arrive in the morning or the afternoon?'
asked Dad.

'It doesn't *matter,*' said Jack. 'And I'm not
telling you any more because
I'm going to bed.'

A week passed and Jack ate lunch with Tashi every day. And every day he heard a marvellous adventure.

He heard about the time Tashi found a ring at the bottom of a pond, and when he put it on his finger he became invisible.

He heard about the time Tashi met a little woman as small as a cricket, and she told him the future.

And he heard about the time Tashi said he
wanted a friend just like Jack, and look! the
fairy had granted his wish.

But at the end of the week he heard the best
adventure of all.

'Listen to what happened to Tashi yesterday,'
Jack said to Mum and Dad at dinner.
'Last night there was a knock at Tashi's door
and when he opened it, guess who was standing
there!'

'Who?' asked Mum.

'The war lord, come to take Tashi back! Tashi turned and ran through the house and out the back door into the garden. He hid under the wings of the swan.'

'Go on,' said Mum.

'Well, the angry war lord chased him out into
the night and when he found the swan he
shouted, "Where did young Tashi go?"

'The swan answered, "If you want to find
Tashi, you must go down to the pond. Drop
this pebble into the water, and when the ripples
are gone you will see where Tashi is hiding."'

'Did the war lord find the pond?' asked Mum.
'Well,' said Jack, 'it was like this. The war lord
did as the swan told him and dropped the
pebble into the pond. But when the water was
still again, he didn't see Tashi. Instead he saw
his own country, and his own palace, and he
saw all his enemies surrounding it, preparing to
attack.

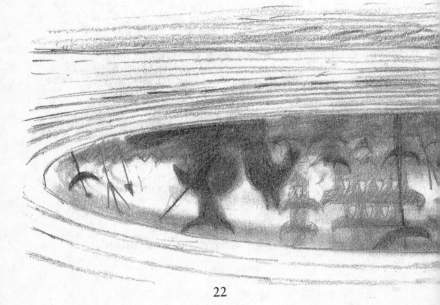

'The war lord was very upset by what he'd seen in the pond and he said to the swan, "I must go home at once!"

'"I will take you," said the swan. "Just climb on my back." And bending his head under his wing he whispered, "Goodbye Tashi, I am homesick for my country. Just stay in the long grass, and he won't see you. Goodbye."'

'Can I bring Tashi home tomorrow to play?'
asked Jack.
'Oh, yes,' said Mum and Dad. 'We're dying to
meet Tashi.'

Jack and Tashi sat at the kitchen table, drinking
their juice.

'Would you like to play in the garden now?'
asked Mum.

'Oh, yes!' said Tashi. 'I like gardens.'

'We could look for a dragon to kill,' Jack said
hopefully to Tashi.

'Are there any dragons left in the garden?'
asked Dad.

'You *always* say the wrong thing!' said Jack.

'He's right though,' said Tashi as they closed the
door behind them. 'There aren't any dragons
left in the whole world. Can you guess how I
know?'

'How?' asked Jack.

'Well, it was like this. Come and I'll tell you about the time I tricked the last dragon of all.'

DRAGON BREATH

Jack took Tashi outside to the peppercorn tree. They climbed up to Jack's special branch and when they were sitting comfortably, Jack said, 'Did you really meet a dragon?'

'Yes,' said Tashi, 'it was like this. One day Grandmother asked me to go to the river to catch some fish for dinner.'

'Was this in your old country?' asked Jack.
'Of course,' said Tashi. 'Grandmother doesn't
believe in travel. Anyway, before I set off,
Grandmother warned me, "Whatever you do,
Tashi," she said, "don't go near the steep,
crumbly bank at the bend of the river. The edge
could give way and you could fall in. And," she
added, "keep your eyes open for dragons."'

'*Dragons!*' said Jack. 'What do you do if you meet a dragon?'

'Well, it was like this,' said Tashi. 'I walked across the field to the river and I caught five fish for dinner. I was just putting them into a couple of buckets of water to keep them fresh when I saw a cloud of smoke. It was rising from a cave, further up the mountain.'

'Ooah, did you run away home?' asked Jack.
'Not me,' said Tashi. 'I took my buckets and
climbed up the mountain and there, sitting at
the mouth of the cave, was the biggest dragon
I'd ever seen.'

'Have you seen many?' asked Jack.

'I've seen a few in my time,' said Tashi. 'But not
so close. And *this* dragon made me very cross.

He was chomping away at a crispy, dragon-breath-roasted pig.

'"That's my father's pig you're eating," I said.

'"I don't care," said the dragon. "I needed something to cheer me up."

'"You can't eat other people's pigs just because
you feel like it," I told him.

'"Yes, I can. That's what dragons do."

'So I sat down next to him and said, "Why do you need cheering up?"

'"Because I'm lonely," said the dragon. "There was a time when I had a huge noisy family. We'd spend the days swooping over the countryside, scaring the villagers out of their wits, stealing pigs and geese and grandfathers, and roasting them with our dragon breath.

Then we'd sing and roar all night till the sun
came up. Oh, those were the days!" The dragon
sighed then and I moved back a bit. "But Mum
and Dad grew old and died, and I ate up the
rest of the family. So now I'm the only dragon
left."

'He looked straight at me and his scaly dragon eyes grew slitty and smoky. "A few mouthfuls of little boy might make me feel better," he said.'

'Oh no!' said Jack. 'What happened then?'
'Well, it was like this. I quickly stood up, ready to run, and the water in my buckets slopped out over the side.

'"Look out!" cried the dragon. "Watch your step! Dragons don't like water, you know. We have to be careful of our fire."'

'*Aha!*' said Jack.

'Yes,' said Tashi. 'That gave me an idea. So I
looked him in the eye and said, "You're not the
last dragon, oh no you're not! I saw one only
this morning down by the river. Come, I'll show
you, it's just by the bend."

'Well, the dragon grew all hot with excitement and he followed me down the mountain to the bend in the river. And there it was all steep and crumbly.

'"He can't be here," said the dragon, looking around. "Dragons don't go into rivers."
'"This one does," I said. "Just look over the edge and you'll see him."

'The dragon leaned over and peered down into
the water. And he saw another dragon!
He breathed a great flaming breath. And the
other dragon breathed a great flaming breath.

He waved his huge scaly wing. And the other
dragon waved his huge scaly wing.

'And then the steep crumbly bank gave way and *whoosh!* the dragon slid *splash!* into the river.

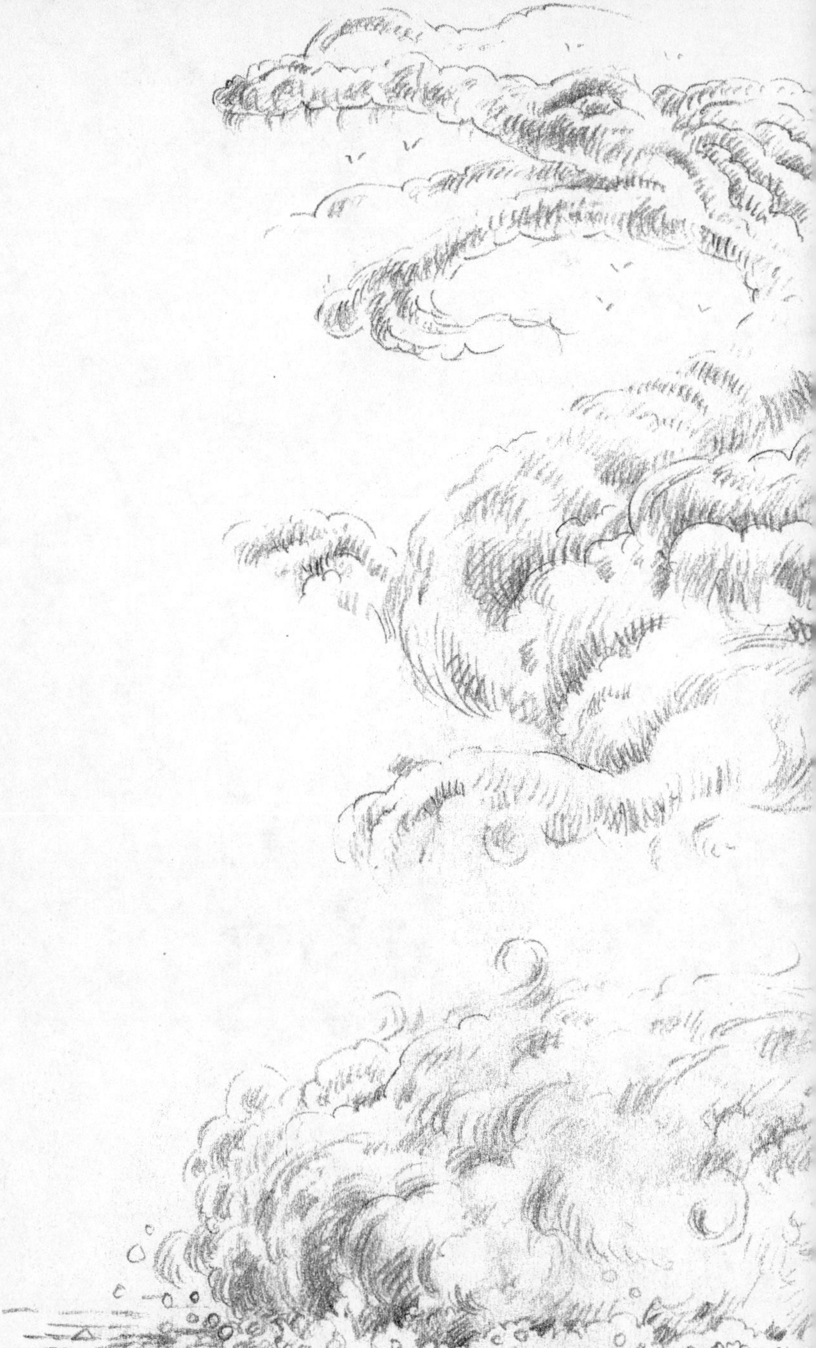

'An enormous dragon-shaped cloud of steam
rose up from the river, and the water sizzled as
the dragon's fire was swallowed up.'

'Hurray!' cried Jack. 'And *then* did you run away home?'

'Yes,' said Tashi. 'I certainly did run home because I was late. And sure enough Grandmother said, "Well, you took your time catching those fish today, Tashi."'

'So that's the end of the story,' said Jack sadly.
'And now all the village was safe and no-one
had to worry any more.'

'Well, it wasn't quite like that,' said Tashi. 'You see, the dragon had just one friend. It was Chintu the giant, and he was as big as two houses put together.'

'*Oho!*' said Jack. 'And Chintu is for tomorrow, right?'

'Right!' said Tashi.

And the two boys slipped down from the tree
and wandered back into the house.